A Lift-the-Flap Book

The
Great
Halloween
Treat

Suzy-Jane Tanner

DAVID BENNETT BOOKS

First published in the United Kingdom in 1999 by David Bennett Books Limited, United Kingdom.
Illustrations copyright © 1996 Suzy-Jane Tanner. Text copyright © 1996 HarperCollins Publishers, United States.
Suzy-Jane Tanner asserts her moral right to be identified as the illustrator of this work.
BRITISH LIBRARY CATALOGUING-IN-PUBLICATION DATA: A catalogue record for this book is available from the British Library.
ISBN 1 85602 297 8
Manufactured in China.

It's Halloween!

Let's go trick-or-treating!

Knock! Knock!
"Trick or treat?"

Knock! Knock!
"Trick or treat?"

Knock! Knock!
"Trick or treat?"

Knock! Knock!
"Trick or treat?"

Knock! Knock!
"Trick or treat?"

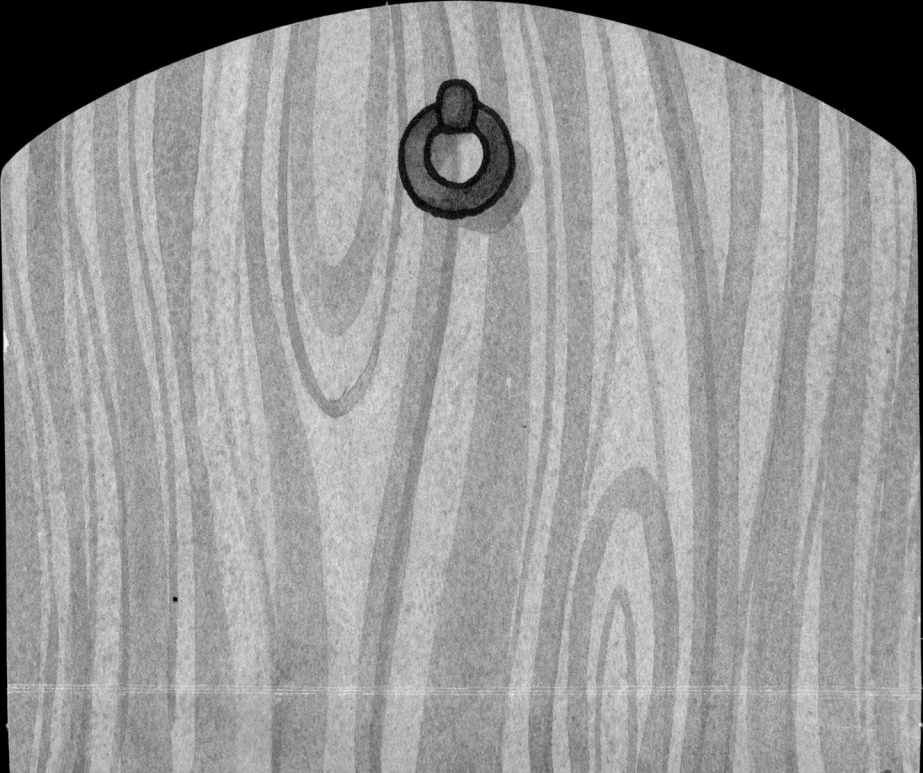

Surprise! We tricked you!
Wasn't that fun?
Come in, there are treats
for everyone!

Knock! Knock!
"Trick or treat?"

Oh no! Here's the last house, and we still don't have any treats.

Happy Halloween, everyone!

The End